OCTOPUS ESCAPES!

Nathaniel Lachenmeyer

Illustrated by Frank W. Dormer

ini Charlesbridge

Welcome to the Aquarium!

← Tickets

Souvenirs →

For Beauty and Wolf Pup, with love—N. L.

To Victoria, always . . .—F. W. D.

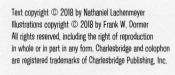

Published by Charlesbridge
85 Main Street, Watertown, MA 02472
(617) 926-0329
www.charlesbridge.com

Printed in China
(hc) 10 9 8 7 6 5 4 3 2 1

Illustrations done in ink with digital color
Display type set in CC Zoinks by Comicraft; Text type set in
    Hooligan JF by Jason Walcott/Jukebox and Alternate Gothic
    No. 1 D by URW•• Design & Development
Color separations by Colourscan Print Co Pte Ltd, Singapore
Printed by 1010 Printing International Limited in Huizhou,
    Guangdong, China
Production supervision by Brian G. Walker
Designed by Martha MacLeod Sikkema

Library of Congress Cataloging-in-Publication Data
Names: Lachenmeyer, Nathaniel, 1969– author. | Dormer, Frank W., illustrator.
Title: Octopus escapes! / by Nathaniel Lachenmeyer; illustrated by Frank W. Dormer.
Description: Watertown, MA : Charlesbridge, [2018] | Summary: Octopus slips out of his tank while the
    aquarium sleeps, teases the animals in the other displays, and leads the security guard on a merry chase.
Identifiers: LCCN 2017042929 (print) | LCCN 2017045906 (ebook) | ISBN 9781632896216 (ebook) | ISBN
    9781632896223 (ebook pdf) | ISBN 9781580897952 (reinforced for library use)
Subjects: LCSH: Octopuses—Juvenile fiction. | Aquarium animals—Juvenile fiction. | Stories in rhyme.
    | Humorous stories. | CYAC: Stories in rhyme. | Octopuses—Fiction. | Aquarium animals—Fiction.
    | Humorous stories. | LCGFT: Stories in rhyme. | Picture books. | Humorous fiction.
Classification: LCC PZ8.3.L1144 (ebook) | LCC PZ8.3.L1144 Oc 2018 (print) | DDC [E]—dc23
LC record available at https://lccn.loc.gov/2017042929

Octopus waits.

Octopus push.

Octopus squoosh.

PLOP!

Aquarium sleeps.

Starfish

Octopus creeps.

Octopus slides.

Octopus hides.

Tentacles swish.

Octopus splash.

Octopus dash.

Octopus bounce.

BOING!

Octopus bowls.

Octopus rolls.

STRIKE!

Sharp teeth clink!

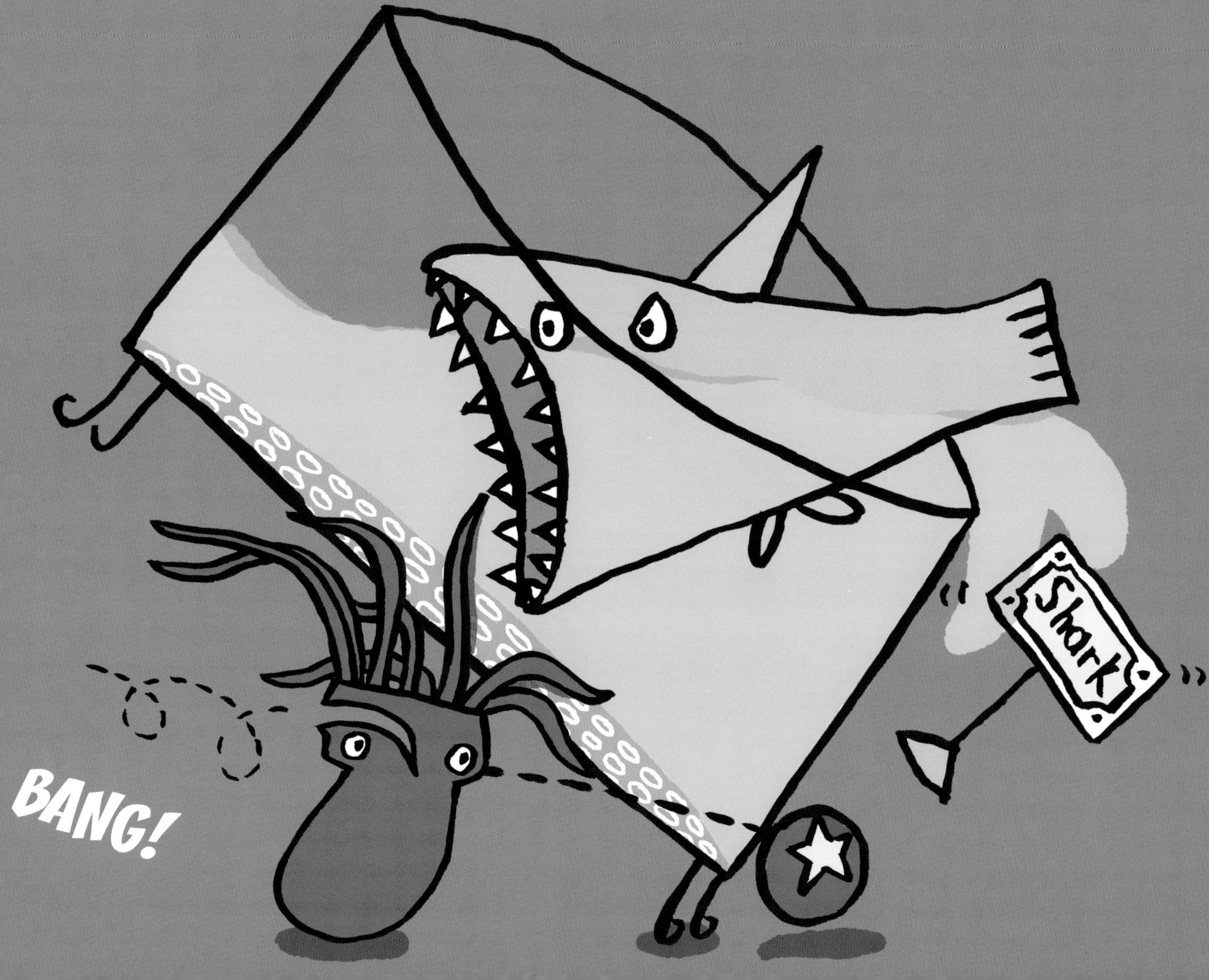

Octopus streaks.

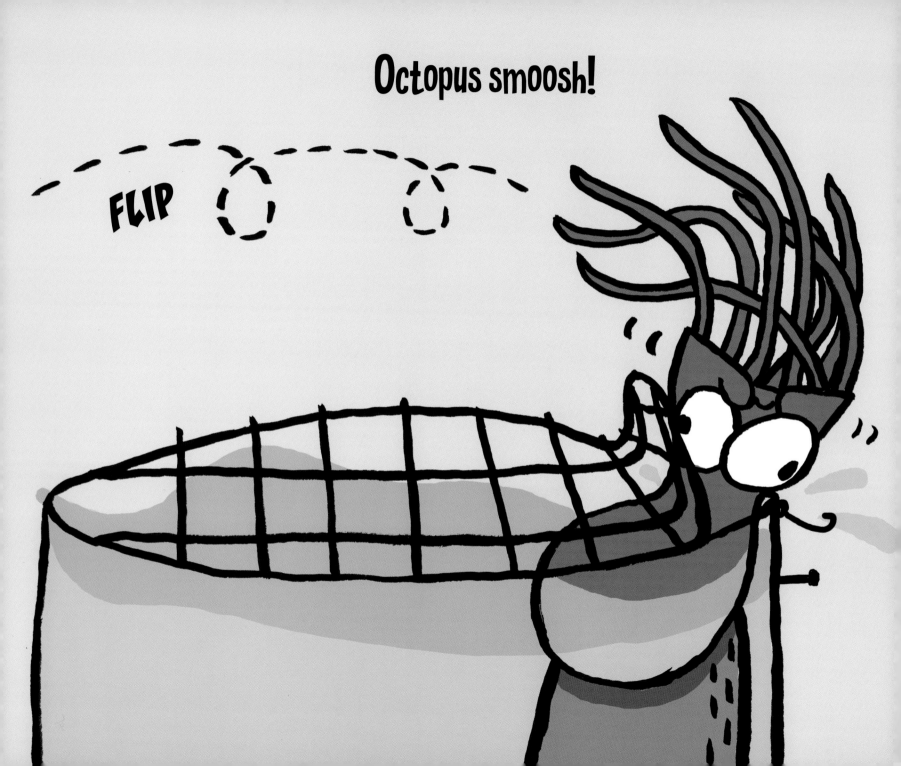

Octopus whoosh!

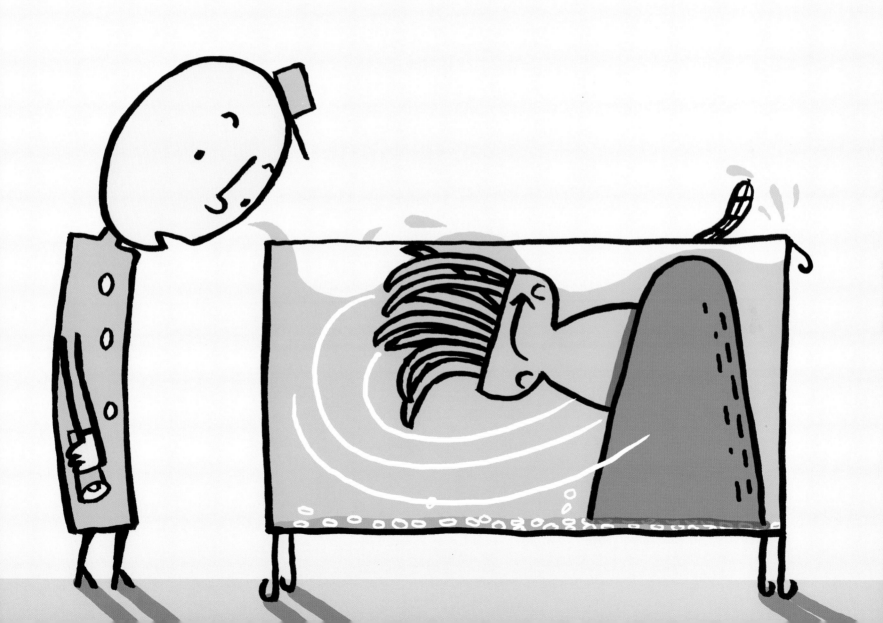

New day begins.

Octopus grins.

Octopus Amazes!

What animal is nocturnal, uses jet propulsion to swim backward, and has eight tentacles, three hearts, blue blood, and a beak? The amazing octopus!

Octopuses are the most intelligent of all invertebrates. Like people, they are playful and curious and have the ability to problem solve. Recently scientists have discovered that some octopuses even use tools. In Indonesia there is a species of octopus that carries coconut shells around to build a portable shelter.

Octopuses are well-known for their extraordinary talent as escape artists. Because their beak-like mouth is the only hard part of their body, octopuses are able to squeeze through tiny openings. Octopuses use their strong tentacles to explore and investigate the world around them. Each tentacle is covered with special suction cups that allow the octopus to taste objects just by touching them.

From time to time, octopuses at aquariums have escaped and gone exploring. For example, at the Brighton Aquarium in England in the 1870s, the resident octopus would escape every night and dine on other exhibits before returning home. After many fish mysteriously disappeared, the octopus was finally caught in the act. In 2016 an octopus at the National Aquarium of New Zealand managed to slip out of its tank, crawl through a 164-foot drainpipe, and escape to the sea.

Octopuses have many clever ways of avoiding predators (such as sharks!). They can squirt ink to distract and confuse their enemies. They can change color and shape to blend in with their surroundings. Some species of octopus even mimic the shape and behaviors of other animals to scare off predators.

What animal is venomous, decorates its den with seashells, can grow a new tentacle if one is lost, and uses its rotating eyes to see right-side up even when upside down? You guessed it. The amazing octopus!

CLICK!